**DO NOT REMOVE
CARDS FROM POCKET**

✓

I thought I heard...

Produced by
Aladdin Books Ltd.
28 Percy Street
London W1P 0LD

Designed by
David West Children's Book Design

First published in the United States in 1996 by
Copper Beech Books
an imprint of
The Millbrook Press
2 Old New Milford Road
Brookfield, Connecticut 06804

Library of Congress Cataloging-in-Publication Data
Baker, Alan.
I thought I heard – / written and illustrated by Alan Baker.
p. cm.
Summary: Because a young girl imagines that spooky things make the sounds she hears in the
dark at bedtime, she is relieved to find the real cause of each sound.
ISBN 0-7613-0460-6 (lib.bdg.). – ISBN 0-7613-0484-3 (trade)
[1. Fear of the dark–Fiction. 2. Bedtime–Fiction. 3. Sound–Fiction.] I. Title.
PZ7.B1688Iag 1996
[E]–dc20   95-43118
CIP   AC

Printed in Belgium

I thought I heard...

Alan Baker

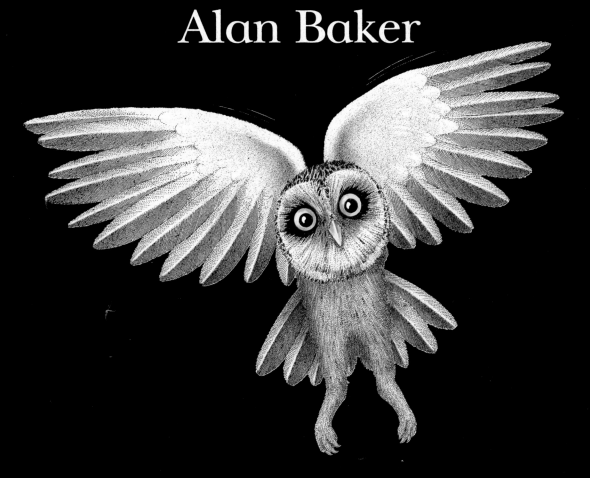

COPPER BEECH BOOKS • BROOKFIELD, CONNECTICUT

I thought I heard a goat's small hooves *tap, tap, tapping* to my door.

It really was...

... a moth's pale wings beating against the windowpane.

I thought I heard the eerie

Whoooooᵒᵒ

of a night owl in the darkness.

It really was...

the wild wind whistling down my chimney,

I thought I heard the

click, click, click

of a beetle.

It really was...

... my bedroom clock ticking away the night.

I thought I heard the *squeak, squeak* of a big, gray mouse.

It really was...

... the hinges on my creaky bedroom door.

I thought
I heard the

hissss

of a slithery,
slimy snake.
It really was...

... my bubbly water fizzing from its bottle.

I didn't see the lightning flash but I thought I heard the thunder

It really was...

... my wooden blocks tumbling from the bookcase.

I thought I heard the *rustling* of a bat's wings in my quilt.

It really was...

... my pet cat Kitty, playing in the wastebasket.

I thought I heard the

buzz, buzz, buzz

of a giant bumblebee.

It really was...

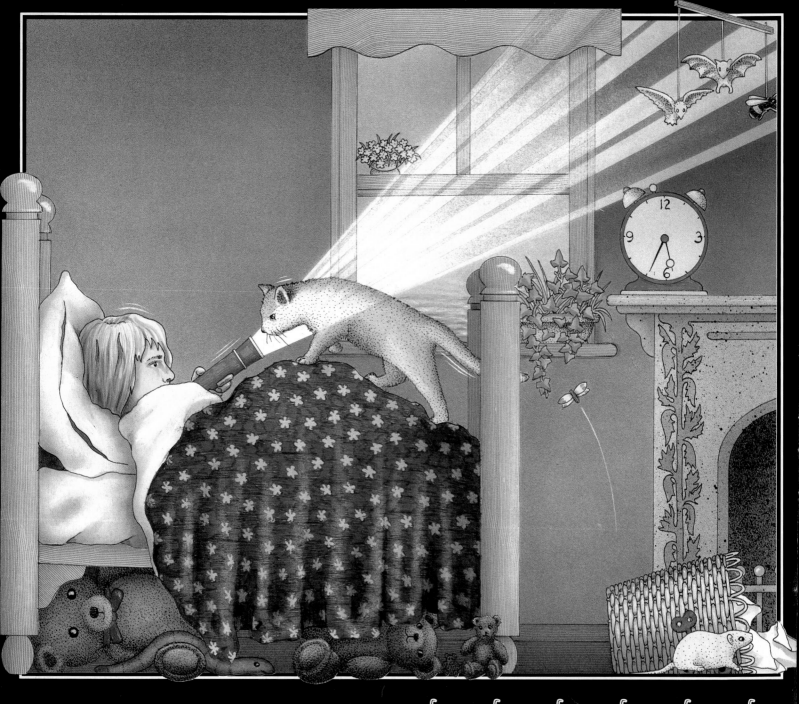

... Kitty, purring on my bed.

I thought I heard the soft

meow

of a playful, sleepy cat.

It really was.

Here are the noises I thought I heard.

squeak, squeak

meow

rustling

Whoooooo

crash

click, click, click

tap, tap, tapping

hissss

buzz, buzz, buzz

What were they really?